T0154882

SCHOOL FOR GIRLS

Ariane Lessard

SCHOOL FOR GIRLS

Translated from the French by
Frances Pope

QC FICTION

Revision: Peter McCambridge
Proofreading: Elizabeth West
Book design: Folio infographie
Cover & logo: Maison 1608 by Solisco
Cover art: Getty Images
Fiction editor: Peter McCambridge

ISBN 978-1-77186-291-2 pbk; 978-1-77186-292-9 epub; 978-1-77186-293-6 pdf

Legal Deposit, 4th quarter 2022
Bibliothèque et Archives nationales du Québec
Library and Archives Canada

Published by QC Fiction, an imprint of Baraka Books
Printed and bound in Québec

Trade Distribution & Returns
Canada - UTP Distribution: UTPdistribution.com
United States & World - Independent Publishers Group: IPGbook.com

Société de développement des entreprises culturelles
Québec 💠💠

Financé par le gouvernement du Canada
Funded by the Government of Canada | Canadä

We acknowledge the financial support for translation and promotion of the Société de développement des entreprises culturelles (SODEC), the Government of Québec tax credit for book publishing administered by SODEC, the Government of Canada, and the Canada Council for the Arts.

life plays in the plaza
with the self I never was

— Alejandra Pizarnik,
"Woman with Eyes Wide Open"
translated from the Spanish by Cecilia Rossi

ghostly young girls breathing cold basement air
(How deep down were we
when we disappeared?)

— Carole David, *The Year of My Disappearance*
translated from the French by Donald Winkler

FALL

ARIANDRE

It isn't the first time that Dame Dominique has cautioned me. She saw me push Annette and run to hide behind the shed. This is where Dame Dread does all the maintenance work on the main yard, repairing the fence, the paving stones that get slippery when it rains. It rained a lot in the last few weeks. The ground loses its shape without roots to hold it in place. The carpet of moss is soaked through with brown-looking water, here behind the shed. I imagine rakes, shovels, wheelbarrows, and other rusty metal tools are kept in there. I can't be sure. Dame Dread, the caretaker, never lets us in. All I can see in the shed is rolls of sheet metal patched with rust, and the shingles that Dame Dread scrupulously repairs in the fall, ready for the coming winter. I pushed Annette because she's a fool. She fell in the mud and her long dress got in the way so she couldn't get up again. The way she follows me around seeking my approval, it was driving me round the bend. I've often glared at her, telling her with my eyes to stay away from me, but she always comes back. I don't need a little sister, I don't even need a friend, I'm perfectly fine on my own. Anyway, nothing she does is worth anyone's attention. Hidden behind the shed, I look at the moss growing along the edge of the stone wall. It's squashy and my feet sink into it. I like plants. I like how they smell, how they surround and cover. You can't get away from them. Behind the shed is the forest. Once the snow starts to fall, I shall probably miss the woods. Everything will be different then. This is where I hide, behind the shed. Before, it was where the other Catherine used to come. I'm standing in her footsteps. Dame Dominique came and found me, shook me out of my thoughts. She put her hand on my forehead and told me to come back to class. Dame Dominique sets me straight. She knows I'm bright. In Literature, it's my writing she likes the best—its ebb and flow, she says. That's what you would hear if you could listen to people's secret thoughts. All of it veined with mystery, creeping in until it's all around you.

CORINNE

Before I came here, I lived with my parents and my brothers, away down the lane. In a farm village that smelled of manure. Fields, everywhere fields. Dirt lanes bordering them, sky over half the horizon. Blue and yellow. We'd drive down the dirt lanes on a horse and cart. Our wheels carved out tracks, and on our way back, the tracks got a little deeper. Our wheels showed the way we'd gone. You could see every trip we made, just by looking at the churned-up dirt behind us. House to village. House to forest. Then, finally, house to boarding school. After that, there were no more outings on the horse and cart. Sometimes they came to fetch me in the summer. My brothers are still carving up the land. But I have lost the freedom to come and go, the lanes. I don't move anymore. I'm rooted here at the window. The girls at the boarding school go walking. They go into the forest, which has no door but a thousand doors. I don't go roaming around there. I stay on familiar paths. Walk on habitable ground. I'd like to turn into a boy, go back to the hamlet, drive the horse and cart. I'd like to go back to the village on the horse and cart and turn into a boy. If I had that, dangling between my legs, would my father let me come home? If mine were on the outside, could I go back to my brothers? All I have is this hole. This hole means I can't go home. This hole brought me to the boarding school. This hole. I would stop it up.

COLETTE

Corinne is my friend my best friend. She has long sharp nails like a cat. With her long nails, she scratched Jeanne's hands, drew blood, while we were playing Devil's Tail in the main hall. You have to go behind people and steal their tail their cloth tail. Corinne came to take mine, but Jeanne stole hers, so she scratched her. Jeanne's hands bled and the blood ran down onto the floor of the main hall, it ran like that drip drip. Dame Anne who teaches mathematics came and stopped the game. After recess we played on our own, Corinne and me, in my little bedroom up under the eaves. We play often with our feet. I sit on this side of the bed. Corinne sits on that side. I tickle her with the ends of my toes. First on the soles of her feet, then the crook of her knees when she's lying on her front. It's nice. I tap her on the bottom with the sole the sole of my foot. Then I slip my toes up to. I try to slide my foot into. She's the one who showed me. I wouldn't do it with anyone else but Corinne, I would only do it with her.

JEANNE

my pulse jumped in my palm
my pulse jumped in my whole hand
my pink cheeks in the mirror
my reflection blurred in my hand's deep lines
flatten the pedal of the sink
my blood in stars in the fountain
pulse
dame anne takes me to the nurse
her hands on my martyr

CORINNE

I smile as I follow Jeanne's trail out of the main hall. Dame Dread hands me the mop. It's not my job to clean up her drops. The red water oozes over the tiles. The red water gets stuck between the cracks in the floor. I kept my cloth tail, took it back to my bedroom up under the sloping roof, rolled it up in a ball and slipped it into my pants. If it weren't for the older girls, I would be king.

LÉA

Science class is in the basement where the floors, washbasins, and stairs are made of concrete. A house reflected upside down. The whole basement seems to have sunk into the ground. They made the cellar deeper and put the basement there. When you go down, you don't feel the sun anymore, there's only the light coming through two windows. Nothing leaks, nothing escapes. Every room has two lightwells that get blocked in winter. Then, Dame Gabrielle sends us out a few times a week to shovel the courtyard—for her mood, she says. When you put your hand on the dusty floor, the concrete is cold and damp. The ground has started to freeze. And always that dreadful feeling, the further you go into the cellar. In the dark, but in the light too, the feeling of going quietly down to your own grave. The rooms around the science classroom are workshops. A printing room used by the older girls, with tiny letters scattered across the desks. And the press for when our stories are fixed. In the other corner, the laundry room and the dresses that hang from the ceiling like ghosts, to dry. In the darkness at the end of the corridor, there's the vault with its heavy metal door. A sarcophagus. At every bend of the corridor that borders the inner courtyard, I imagine seeing a ghost. Or just a pair of eyes. Just for a second, during a class—catching a glimpse of something. I often have the impression that I'm being watched. Even though it feels unreal, thinking of death still frightens me every time I go down the stairs and get the dry, earthy smell of the concrete in my nose. I keep going down there alone, despite my fears. If someone were there. If some dead soul were to come and carry me off to harm me. That Léa with her soft skin and her orifices. I say that I'm afraid, but it's a pleasant fear. It's also an expectation. A morbid expectation. Maybe the last girls are watching us from the other side of the wall.

FRÉDÉRIQUE

In the dining hall, I sit between Catherine and Diane. I like to go around with them because we look good together, dare I say. And if someone wanted to take a photograph of us, I would sit in between them and put my arms around their shoulders, to show that we are friends. We eat the meals that Dame Françoise makes for us, that she cooks so well. Her hands are always grubby from something—the garden, the rake, the beets. They chose Dame Françoise to do the cooking because of her maternal instinct. She had a daughter once, but she had to give her up for adoption. It seems that it happened a lot, back then. It's been twenty years now, she says. Her daughter is older than we are. It must be wonderful to be an only child. It is good of her to feed us, when deep down she must be thinking about all the times she couldn't feed her daughter. I am happy that Catherine became my friend because Diane's silence was starting to bother me, dare I say. She has always shut herself up in silence. But after a while, you need people around you who talk, otherwise all you hear is the wind whistling between the old bricks. Benoîte, my sister, is with the older girls. When we're at the school, it's as if we had nothing to do with one another. It's only in summer that we meet again at our parents' house. And then I make the most of Benoîte's company because I know it won't last long. I never know what my sister thinks of me. The first snow fell yesterday, and it got mixed up with the dead leaves that smell of leaf-mould and rain.

DIANE

As being ordinary As being dead As we think of
it As we cut the bread As we go down the stairs
As we eat at last As we straighten the stone slabs
As we pick an apple As we dance As we can read
As we look at the stars As we light the candles As
the other house As we might say As we appear
As we sing As once As the skipping rope As next
to it As the wind bites As the time passes As if
I were there As if I could leave As if the wind
sings As if the call As the other Catherine As
if tomorrow morning As if the woods As if the
words As if the dead As we go down As we go for
a walk As we love to pray As if I were As if I went
As if I became As the soap cracks As the cuts

As my knife As I work hard As if I were sinking As if I were swimming As if I didn't exist As we explain As we understand mathematics As we remain As we change As wolves As we write As we mark ourselves As we disappear As we return from between the stones

ANNETTE

red leaves fall and fall and are cleared up with the
rake scrape scrape raked into big piles for jumping I jump in now we have to start over dame
dread sends me knives with her eyes ariandre too
and laure she smiles she understands more than
the others the joy i want to grab the rake out of
ariandre's hands to fix the mountain she doesn't
like me she wants to see me hang she wants to
see me lost in the forest soon i'll go and get lost
to make them happy i'll get lost deep in the forest
further than the falls annette poor annette dear
annette sweet little child found no welcome from
anyone no warmth lost in the woods the birds are
my only friends i watch them at the bird-feeder a

great dance of wings to catch the biggest meal in
beaks split open crammed and scatter the smaller
birds terrified little jumps little feet then wing-
beats up to the trees waiting their turn when
the big birds with split open beaks fly off the
little ones come back to eat the crumbs and the
hummingbirds feed at another feeder and no one
else can steal their little honey drink because no
one else has the right beak i am a hummingbird
and I eat apart from the rest it's cold now that
the trees are sleeping goodbye last colours the
blackness beauty falls and dame dread looks at
me like a knife

ARIANDRE

I wonder if I've done something I ought not to have done. I can't always understand my mistakes. I can't always control my spirits. The words that come out of my mouth aren't always good. My actions aren't always nice and polite. I have an insect that takes over. An insect that blurs the boundaries. What's the right thing. What will turn others against me. My insect flies around in my head and only stops when it wants to. It makes me pull other girls' hair. Throw dirt in their eyes, shove Annette. It makes me lie. It makes me invent stories that only I know are not true. I fell off the swing and I cut my arm on the chain. I told Dame Anne the nurse that it was a cat. When she cleaned the cut, the insect buzzed in circles at the back of my head. I went back on the swing. Look, I'm wounded! I wonder if the other Catherine held it against me. If it was all my fault that she left us, Laure and me, that she had had enough. Every time I go back and stand in the moss, I tell myself, she sees me. I preferred the old Catherine to the new one. The first one to the false one. Today, the moss split under my weight. I saw Diane in the woods, her arms around a tree.

BENOÎTE

We're the top class, the eldest girls. Our bedrooms are separate from the younger girls' bedrooms, with the mistresses in between. Thérèse
and Sylvie are twins but they don't look alike.
Charlotte, Dorothée, and Lucile are cousins, and
they help Dame Françoise with the garden when
there's no snow, and with the cooking. Rose-Anna
has a lover from town who visits her at her house
in the village in summer. She tells us everything.
Aimée and Suzanne paint with me. We do oil
paintings in the inner courtyard, or in the little
room next to the language classroom that we've
made our own. Bernadette comes to join us in the
evenings after she's shut up the printing room

with Jacinthe, who goes off to bed. We've made a little in-group for those who like the arts and who want to focus on them at school. The mistresses, especially Dame Dominique, have nothing against it because we're mature and we know how to take care of ourselves. Our canvases are framed and hung on the walls, on the landings of the younger girls' floor and our own, when they meet the approval of Dame Dominique, our language teacher. Jacinthe doesn't paint anymore, not now that her sister Louise is with the last girls. Four winters ago, it was.

CATHERINE

Dame Dominique teaches languages and elocution. She writes in flowing lines on the blackboard, chalking out words that we copy down. I saw a brachycera. I. Saw. A. Brachycera. Brachycera. She repeats the words so we understand them. A brachycera. I carefully form the letters in my writing pad, holding my pencil lightly the way Dame Dominique taught us. I never squeeze the pencil between my fingers, and I never smudge the paper under my hands. I like to keep my hands clean. Some girls don't want to please Dame Dominique. I don't understand. It's good to do things the right way. To do things immaculately.

CORINNE

I saw a brachyssera. Brachycera. I always add one letter too many, in all the possibilities of spelling. The writing on the blackboard is a trace, too. A trace left behind, marking the way, girls who write badly won't go anywhere in life. I struggle to form the Os. Curves don't lead anywhere. I prefer things that go straight ahead. Parallel lines, or angles. Jeanne had a bandage around her hand. Jeanne is too soft, and she'll pay for it in life. I'd have liked to see her wound. I hurt her. I hurt her to win, to show her that you don't win without your tail. You don't win without that roll of cloth in your underwear. You don't win without the help of the devil in your pants.

COLETTE

I saw a brachyssera. Brachycera. It's Corinne's fault I got it wrong. We sit next to each other, and in front of us Jeanne and Laure share a desk, and behind us Léa and Ariandre never so much as look at each other. Catherine has taken Diane's place her place next to Frédérique, and Diane sits in front of Dame Dominique with little Annette. We are the younger class. The older girls have science when we have languages, and mathematics when we have science. We see them eating at the older girls' table, and they sit watching us, at the younger girls' table. We hardly ever speak to each other. We are aged between ten and fifteen, and they, between sixteen and twenty. We hardly talk to the women they are becoming, but their hands their hands are beautiful. Benoîte is Frédérique's older sister, more beautiful than Frédérique.

LAURE

we're afraid of her yes because of the paving
                              stones hee hee

she spends the fall replacing them yes

so we won't find out

that's where they sleep

damedread

ARIANDRE

I don't understand why Annette thinks she can be my friend. I didn't ask to hold hands with anyone. I hold hands with myself now. I hold hands with a tree, I hold hands with the rolls of toilet paper in the lavatories, I hold hands with the corridors and the desks. Especially the desks in the mathematics classroom. The radiators make them warm. I put my hand on the radiator sometimes, and I only pull it away when it's hot, when it's burning. I notice that I'm slowly losing the feeling in the tips of my fingers. It's a good thing to lose. I have a callous on the knuckle of my right index finger from holding my pencil too tight. I gnaw it with my teeth. It's as if my eleventh finger were growing there. The nail on my ring finger grows more quickly than the rest. The other girls don't notice things like that. Every time I put it in my nose, I bleed. That, they notice.

CATHERINE

The main hall is wooded with pillars. There are even pillars in its centre. A cathedral of columns that mirrors the forest. We do handstands up against them. Ariandre always keeps her head down for too long. The blood rushes to her head, and her eyes end up all red. That girl never does anything normal. Why must she insist on doing things backwards? When someone kicks a ball in the main hall, you can bet it will bounce back and hit Annette in the face. She has a face that attracts balls. Or that attracts the ball that attracts the foot that attracts the person who wants to kick it in her face. I don't always notice who's kicking, since I'm hiding behind the pillars. I wouldn't want my pretty nose to get hit.

FRÉDÉRIQUE

Diane never eats her fill. In mathematics, Diane rests her head on her hands. Her head has gotten too heavy. Her wrists are thin, and her ankles too. She won't undress with us in the changing room before we go to play in the main hall. She's adrift in her uniform, dare I say. But I shan't mention it to Catherine—she'll only start to bad-mouth Diane, just like she did with the others. When Catherine decides another girl isn't good enough, she stops talking to her. She did that with Laure, she did that with Ariandre, and if she does that with Diane then soon it will be my turn, and I couldn't bear that. Catherine is like my sister, dare I say.

ANNETTE

from my window under the eaves the forest open-
ing up trees bare warm inside rows of pines that
go on forever walking in the rays of light that slip
through walking with the sound crack toward the
river silent calm the ground for sleeping in the
winter calm the bears with their secrets calm the
dames for our suppers dame dread watching us
in the forest my nest

COLÉTTE

Benoîte is with the older girls she has the chest
the chest of a woman. I would like her to take me
in her arms and press my head gently against her
bosom. I would like to hear her heart beating, my
ear to her ribs. I would like her to stroke my hair
slowly, to stroke my back. Give me shivers shivers
down my spine. Corinne is not someone to confide in. I don't confide in Corinne, I would rather
have Benoîte take care of me. I would like it if she
talked to me and knew that I would be her little
cat if she wanted. I would go with the older girls
to the printing workshop and I would write the
most beautiful love letter to Benoîte.

JEANNE

when to stop clenching my fist to stop the scabs
                                      from breaking

keep my palm open
at all times
i ask diane to be my right hand
diane is with me and meanwhile laure is
                                      in the shed
only dame anne knows that i scratch off
                                      my scabs
to keep the trace
of my violence under her ointment

LAURE

through the window girls learning new kinds
of science

you have to learn yes or you have to just know
hee hee

they don't know that something is brewing
in the earth

an ending that starts with the roof

but i know that those good sciences are dead

the headmistress has left hee hee

48

before it all turns upside down

damedread tells me yes she shows me in her
                                          metal pot

soon the road will be impassable

DIANE

I do not know Annette I do not know Laure I do
not know Léa I do not know Frédérique I do not
know Catherine I do not know Dame Gabrielle
I do not know Corinne I do not know Colette I do
not know Dame Dominique I do not know Dame
Françoise I do not know Jeanne I do not know
the other Catherine I do not know Dame Anne
I do not know Benoîte Thérèse Charlotte Sylvie
Lucile Bernadette Jacinthe Suzanne Rose-Anna
Aimée Dorothée the eldest girls I do not know the
headmistress I do not know Dame Dread I do not
want to know her I only know the one who writes
and what she comes up with cannot be trusted

COLETTE WOULD HAVE SAID

A blank I am without Corinne and I make myself a blank. The story of my disappearance starts when Corinne gets into the cart and sets off down the road and her brothers welcome her and her family surrounds her. I cannot leave with them I am not her friend. I am just Colette and she tramples on me because she can. She tried to trample over the others before me over their back like a doormat. That's where she wipes her feet. She takes herself for a boy who has the right to wipe his feet. To slough off his dirtiness and muck up the girls' clothes that they go to wash together in the river. My back is broad enough so I offer it to anyone who wants to take a turn.

ARIANDRE

At heart, I'm not a bad person. I've just learned to unlearn good manners. They only serve one purpose, anyway, and that's to stop anything new from being created. The dames prevent new things by keeping all the girls closed in, surrounded, beholden. But I'm not someone who can be shut in. With four walls around me, my mind wanders outdoors. I think about going to stand in the moss, I think about going to look inside the shed. I saw Laure going in there one day, and soon after, Dame Dread went inside too. I didn't dare look in through the windows. I said to myself, looking is not allowed. I said to myself, Ariandre, perhaps you ought not to. I stamped on the moss instead, the way I like to, and my boots sucked up lots of water. I didn't see. Didn't look. Power slipped away. What is Laure going to do in the shed? Snow fell again today and lay on the ground like a carpet.

LAURE

i don't know much i don't know anything i don't
know the meaning of mathematics the meaning
of a clock face there's only one thing i can do and
that's to leave the class yes

but i know flowers and i know plants and i know
herbs and i know ice and snow and i know the
future under the windows yes

only the mad speak with a grain of truth hee hee

LÉA

Dame Anne says that few women take the mathematical route. That she often had to work much harder than the men who studied with her. She went to a school for adults, a mixed school. I would give anything to go to a school with boys. I would stare at them in lessons and learn nothing but the line of their jaw. If Dame Anne knew what I think about, she would be ashamed to find me so crude. If the dead watch us, if their spirits see inside our heads, well then, I'm destined for eternal damnation. That Léa, she only wants one thing and it's a bad thing. She wants to be cursed with a kick in the belly. When I can't sleep, I get out of bed. Being very careful not to cross Dame

Dread on her night rounds, I go down the stairs to the cellar. At the end of the chilly corridor where my frozen feet skim the floor, I open the door to the science classroom. From my desk, I take out a screwdriver that Laure stole from the shed, and I slip the handle up between my legs.

WINTER

BENOÎTE WOULD HAVE SAID

The young girls, and the older girls too, who are better, study at the boarding school high on the snowy mountain. When spring comes, the ground will take some time to shed its thick white carpet. The shade of the conifers that surround the school will keep the air cool, and the snow keeps covered up what is freezing, slowly, in the earth. The school stays wrapped in its blanket for nearly six months every year, on account of its northerly position. You might picture it as a dot in the middle of the forest, accessible via a gravel path along which horses and carts can travel in the summer. The boarding school has twenty-one boarders and six members of staff, five of whom stay all year round, while the head-mistress makes her escape. She stayed shut in at the school over a few winters, in the past; now she gets out as soon as the first snow starts to fall. She knows that the atmosphere of the place in winter changes you. Never had she felt so imprisoned, surrounded, watched, than in this place. She knows that between the bricks of the school, there creeps a sickness that no one is shielded from. That's what got Louise and the last girls. She calls it the murmur.

ARIANDRE

Dame Dominique says that writing is what lasts. It survives, as on gravestones, carved in our minds and in our skin. It's etched in our skin like the cuts on Diane's arms. She etches herself so she can't forget. I don't forget anything. I repeat my thoughts while walking from the river to the school, or passing under the arches of the wide corridors of the three upper floors. One arch, Dame Dread and Laure in the shed. Twelve arches, Catherine and the other Catherine. Twenty-three arches, the past, and when it's all stirred up enough, I write it down. I let it go. That way I can make some empty space, and my insect goes to sleep. It falls silent and lies down in my skull, curled up in a knot. There needs to be some respite, otherwise I have to leave the classroom with Laure. Otherwise I have to follow her through the snow, squirming in the cold. Otherwise I breathe but the air is too thin and I cough and I gnaw at my eleventh finger. I often imagine what the others are thinking about. Then I write it down.

DIANE

No noise No trouble No isolation Not on the
roof No deer No knowing why Laure laughs
No need of help No want No hunt No snow No
place to get warm Nowhere No stag No apples
No fish No right No want No kindness No sleep
Not since Not anymore Not under the sheets
No science Not Léa Not crazy No friends No
shovel No light Not in the cellar Not today No
leaves No ice No children No trouble No want
Not tomorrow Not liking Not hungry No gashes
No knowing No walk Not with the knife Not
Laure No paper Not Frédérique Not in a village
Not in the house Not in the bedroom Not sure

CATHERINE

Laure and Ariandre were my friends last year.
We all arrived at the same time, and we got
to know each other quite well. All three of us
are the same age. Others are older or younger,
like Annette. I chose to replace them, though,
because I reached a point where even just thinking about them would make me shudder. There
are pivotal moments like that. When you realize
that certain friendships are no longer worth the
trouble. Too many problems. Too much you have
to give. Frédérique seems better positioned to
help me progress. She is wiser, more adapted to
real life. It's just a shame that she keeps company
with that mute, Diane. I'm now at an age where

I simply can't be friends with strange girls. They remain stuck in one place, and I have long since moved on. Laure attracts attention for the wrong reasons. I've nothing against her, nothing against the fact that she's different, nothing. She has the right to be with us, she has the same rights we do. But I don't believe her attitude in class is the result of any intelligible thought process. Dame Gabrielle, who teaches science, often asks her to leave the classroom if she doesn't want to learn. Laure goes out to shovel snow and we see her at the window that looks out onto the inner courtyard. She watches us and laughs. I simply pretend not to see her. I don't give her the attention she craves. I prefer to save my energy for the exercises that Dame Gabrielle wants us to do. And as for Ariandre, well, better to leave her well alone.

LAURE

it will only be a matter of days yes and then

i pay no heed yes lovely phrase i pay no heed
                                    to new knowledge

it won't save us from the fall hee hee

it condemns us from the window

instead go into the woods with damedread yes

she tells me that in summer

it will finally be time

departure

after a long preparation

LÉA

I've often pictured the scene. It starts with the
face of my neighbour's brother who died two
years ago. He was trampled by a stallion, and
that was the end of his pretty face and everything else with it. I cried a lot, but in secret,
keeping my grief to myself. He was so stoic on
his horse. Tall, wild. He took my hand, once,
jumping over the bank that separated his family's
land from ours. Another week and his number
was up. I often imagine meeting his ghost in the
cellar. It wouldn't be frightening to see him—
more like a good omen, carefully constructed
and well thought out. I think about it sometimes
as I'm falling asleep, or in class, when my eyes

glaze over. I've found a way to block the sounds from entering my ears by playing with the pressure of my eardrums. I am physically present, the others can see me, but I am not really there. I pretend my eyes are open, but in fact, they're looking inwards. That's a place I often go to in class. That's where I see my neighbour, dead two years. Sometimes the teacher asks me for the answer at that very moment and I just say I don't know. I would rather feign ignorance than be shaken out of a dream. These moments belong to me alone. That Léa, she dreams about things under the ground. I think that I am looking forward to the summer. I am looking forward to the sounds from outside. Laure often asks me to walk along the river with her and talk about the dead. I should say yes more often. See the glimmers that make it through the frozen current.

CORINNE

The carts can no longer reach us. Road impassable. I borrow Dame Anne's skis and make circles
around the school. I've had stomach-ache for
the last few days. I hide under the stairs waiting
for Jeanne or Annette or Colette to come down,
then I jump out and scare them. Dame Anne
knows that I need distractions, otherwise I get
nasty and I scratch. I wear myself out in the yard,
tracing lines with my skis carving the snow, and
I don't come back until the end of the day, my
clothes wet. Sweating all that water gives me the
feeling of working. I don't wash right away, I wait
until supper is over so my smell gets everywhere.
I can't stay in the library all afternoon. I can't stay

shut in with the others and their quiet concen-
tration. Their silence grates on me. I spend too
much time thinking about how to destroy them.
I bring my stench to the dining hall. Colette will
go and sit with someone else.

LAURE

hee hee when you step into the shed you can
                                        breathe yes

i am the only one who can enter the hidden
garden

without damedread throwing me out hee hee

the plants trail like snakes there in secret

to heal minds

i make my way across the white stones

on my way to the shed

ARIANDRE

I'll put Annette under the stones before long. I was at the big table in the library, writing, and I could see Annette spying on me from behind the English novels. The minute I went to catch her out, that nosey girl, she pretended to be looking for a book. Everyone knows Annette doesn't read English novels. Too busy daydreaming. She had just better leave me alone, since I can't escape outside anymore. If she doesn't start respecting the solitude I need for my writing—and soon—I shan't be held responsible for my actions. She wouldn't be the first to find out what I can do.

ANNETTE

the snow fell and dame anne with it and the roof
lost its snow and dame anne lost her leg and since
then we don't have mathematics it's good some
say it's good that dame anne crippled herself that
her leg smashed into a thousand pieces crack that
we saw from the window of the science room that
looks out onto the inner courtyard we saw the
snow falling and dame anne after it that from the
very top of the wall dame anne fell it's not nice to
laugh until you're crying it's not nice to say why
not on her neck dame françoise takes care of the
leg that's swollen up that's so big it looks like my
body that's so twisted it looks like a tree trunk
dame anne screams and her screams can be heard

from the cellar all the way up to the bedrooms under the eaves she screams and the birds fly away amongst her screams there are words that dame dominique wouldn't want us to learn from the suffering mouth of dame anne who twists around like her leg dame dread tries to apply the plaster but dame anne couldn't care less about the orders of dame dominique who tells her to quieten down dame anne cries out and no one has ever known her that way it's a real sight she opens her legs wide and kicks with her foot that's not black then dame dread makes her drink a special brew and dame anne disappears goodbye

LAURE

damedread says go and pick deadly nightshade

quickly quickly before the screams turn
                                    to poison

the snow kills what lives

in the shed our life-saving reserves

CATHERINE WOULD HAVE SAID

Heal my mistress, heal her quickly otherwise I will despair, I will have lost my guide. If authority dies, I am not worth a single candle.

ARIANDRE

All we hear is Dame Anne's cursing. One more agonized soul for my stories. Lack of sleep is nothing new to me, I know the fatigue of the small hours. It's funny to notice, though, how quickly the others have grown used to Dame Anne's lamentations. Like a baby we all have to take care of. Dame Françoise has started to enjoy it, she can pretend that she is looking after Dame Anne as she would have looked after the child they took away from her. She can tell herself she's finally got a hand in someone's survival, even if the only truly helpful thing would be to carry Dame Anne out to a cabin at the edge of the forest. Best to leave her there. And Dame

Françoise could go back to fantasizing in the kitchen. Maybe then, finally, all those who are used to sleeping at night could get back to normality. I see their look, their dark-circled eyes that say, something has to give. I see Diane trying to say, with her face that doesn't dare speak, that she's worn out from hearing the screams. Dame Anne doesn't belong to the world of good manners anymore. She has turned wild, and now I slip into her room to sponge her feverish brow as soon as Dame Dread leaves, having poured her concoction into Dame Anne's mouth. That's the moment the screams stop, the same moment she starts to talk furiously, vehemently, about her life before. She talks about flies, she talks about open windows, she talks about food on the table and the flies that have no shame. I take note of everything that comes out of her generous mouth.

DIANE

the first time i speak it's the first time i speak
laure came to my room gave me a special drink
good for you diane i am in summer i am here the
stars pour out of my eyes and go back slowly into
the sky sparkling the needles of the trees clink
together iced over the crust of the snow cracks
under my weight i am afraid but my body has
gone cold i saw huge antlers followed them the
sounds of the wind my skin absorbs the smells i
feel the wood the warm fur and i rub my face in
it sounds come out of me and i am a she-moose i
breathe in the beautiful animal that lets me climb
on its back and we gallop the pine trees whip
my face and the needles taste of the forest and

i fly up to the stars from my eyes in the sky i see the school tiny in the midst of the whiteness my mouth is full of snow i bite on it in the sky bite on the clouds and the birds with new sensations my hair full of ice my throat frozen in laughter possessed smile piercing through my teeth through my windpipe cleansing me of all my memories i touch the moon then my hands disappear i lose my fist and i fall into a house i had forgotten pale walls clammy hands my twin moving the arch of the back walking to another forest from the past ridiculous humility she meets a mother and her children As if I were lying As if I were becoming As if the memories As if it were the end

JEANNE

this morning in the bath tub fast asleep
leaves and branches
in diane's hair

on her cheeks
and her forehead scratches
tiny lines etched
in the whiteness of her skin

ANNETTE

dame anne continues to scream every night she
says we live in an abyss and it's not a world and if
she'd known she never would have come all the
way out here ariandre drinks it all in the secret
sweating behind the closed door the roof is thick
with snow and no one wants to go up there again
laure has shovelled the snow from the windows
in the courtyard she shovelled the pink snow of
dame anne's leg put it in a box threw it in the
frozen river crack the current that's left carried
away the colour of dame anne goodbye

FRÉDÉRIQUE

Dame Françoise takes us to one side. Diane, Catherine, and me. Let's have a change, my dears, she says. We'll prepare lunch. Normally it's the older girls that help her. She has us follow her down to the cellar. Diane won't go inside. There are sacks full of vegetables that the older girls and Dame Françoise and Dame Gabrielle grew last summer. We have them to thank. The garden is behind the school, rotting under the snow at the edge of the forest. Dame Françoise takes a bag and fills it up, her hands dirty. We come back up to the kitchen. You take the potatoes, you take the turnips, you take the carrots. I see Catherine looking at Diane looking at the potatoes. Dame

Françoise seems glad to have us there with her, dare I say. She sings in a language that Dame Dominique hasn't taught us. She says it comes from the mountain. Dame Françoise takes care of us. She wraps us in her kind arms. She sings us songs so we won't hear the yelling. She says we must smile, and she lets Diane go and sit by the wall on her own. I'm afraid that Diane will do something strange and get on the wrong side of Catherine. We have never peeled vegetables before. Catherine learns fast, watches Dame Françoise closely, copies. She smiles a knowing smile when I ask for help. Catherine is always quick to learn, quick to make friends. Then she won't help anyone else. She never looks back. She pretends to be one of the older girls. She pretends to be Benoîte, dare I say.

ANNETTE

what looks like the end of dame anne looks like
the end of winter looks like something that no
one knows how to finish dame dominique and
dame gabrielle collapse and dame anne's leg is
black up to her thigh a horse's leg you'd say dame
dread pushes me out of the room slams the door
and i hear the women wail the snow will make
her a lovely bed

LAURE

in dame anne's bedroom

a stench of gangrene

the vessel has been emptied yes

the first to fall damedread sighs hee hee

DIANE

Not in the bedrooms Not in the hallway Not in the bathroom Not in the main hall Not in the language classroom Not in the science classroom Not in the kitchen Not in the dining room Especially not in the mathematics classroom Not in the cellar Not in the vault Not in the snow Not on the roof Not in a tree Not in the inner courtyard Not in the library Not at the falls Not at the river and in the shed

FRÉDÉRIQUE WOULD HAVE SAID

Dame Françoise so gentle Dame Françoise so good Dame Françoise dear mother so kind. So lucky to be cared for in the cuckoo's nest.

ARIANDRE

I am strong. I know that when people see me for the first time, I look different, and I catch their eye. I like that. I like to catch people's eye. Even so, there are times when I should like to be invisible—to slowly vanish under the snow, my outline melting away—the better to observe the others. I should like to slip in through every window. Slip into every head and finally understand what's brewing in there, what I spend my time trying to guess. Pity I can do nothing but imagine. I am not like Frédérique, one of those people who thinks she can learn to know. I don't care for time-wasting. I care for invention. I invent. With every fibre of my being, I invent. I knew, when I returned to

Dame Anne's room, that her soul had gone the way of the last girls. I rifled through Dame Anne's possessions. Notebooks full of calculations, only good for the fire. A brooch in the shape of a fly. The green scarf she always tied round her neck. The clothes that weren't contaminated by the awful smell. A couple of dice and playing cards. A few photos with some adults, taken when she was young. It was the brooch that interested me. A strange piece of jewellery.

JEANNE

in a rolled-up blanket
the smell followed dame dread to the shed
on the work bench laure talked
of the white foot and the black foot
i know now that this is my place
here with my shadowy twin
what laure does i copy
the shed is a garden
the better to watch the time pass yes
i look at diane who no longer believes in walking
her cheeks striped by the pines

now i am not the only damaged one

LÉA

I don't go down to the cellar anymore, not since Dame Anne died. I don't want her to see what's in my mind, don't want her to know. To discover all my thoughts from under the ground, with the others that watch. That Léa, she only wants one thing and it's a bad thing. It's too hard to stay here inside these walls where her screams used to be. Her screams still hang in the air that moves between every window. Dame Gabrielle opened them all, despite the cold. But instead of letting out the shadow of Dame Anne, she seems to have let in the shadows of the last girls, who were sleeping deep in the forest.

LAURE

dame anne fell yes

one more under the stone slabs when the snow
melts

another one yes

it's in winter hee hee that they all fall down

learning mathematics isn't the same as learning
to balance

i shovel snow by the science room window
hee hee

LÉA WOULD HAVE SAID

The fear the fear that they see me in the cellar
breathing in the cyprine of my fingers.

SPRING

CORINNE

Lumps of snow fall from the roof with an enormous crash. Every crash is followed by a few seconds of silence in the science class. Dame Gabrielle has developed a twitch. Every time a lump of snow comes away from the rest and falls into the courtyard, she seems to rally all the nerves in her forehead and scrunch them up at the centre. Snow. Twitch. It's funny to watch. Dame Anne's fall repeats in our heads but the suffering has gotten less. We remember the fall because we want to feel it, to convince ourselves that we still feel the pain. The truth is that everyone has slept better since she left, finally, in her rug. Soon enough, the snow on the roof will melt and the girls will start thinking of walks in the forest, of picking fruit in the orchard. But I will think about the road and about my brothers coming to fetch me, to take me away from here. I will finally be gone. I swear, this summer I will make my father forget about sending me back to the boarding school. My breasts are starting to hurt, I think those things are growing. I'm starting to look like the girls in the older class. I'm hideous.

ANNETTE

by the river the bears drink sleep sated they con-
tinue their walk through the trees they cross back
over the river to nose about where the girls live
dame dread has brought out her gun and dame
anne is waiting for the cold to subside so she can
rot laure watches her laure says she kept a lock
of her hair ariandre goes away whenever i come
near her maybe i smell bad maybe i am terribly
ugly or maybe there's something ridiculous and
empty in my face and i look like the crows that
caw and chase away the hummingbirds and wake
us up in the morning but i need ariandre to see
me i want to be in her eyes that look at the trees
otherwise i go back to my feeder alone

ARIANDRE

Some people don't deserve to speak. They deserve to be mute. I wish you could simply touch their throat and all the sound would fade and vanish. Never again could they say things like the things that Catherine or Colette or Frédérique or Léa have said. So caught up in their own existence. They think they have to play a role, to become, to feel they have their place in the world, without fear of losing it. I think a lot of people deserve to be muzzled. That would teach them to think twice before they spoke, to not be despicable. Words aren't good for everyone. Diane worked that out a long time ago. What wouldn't I give to have the old Catherine back. She held her tongue.

JEANNE

dame gabrielle bangs her head against the wall
on her forehead a mark appears
something's off with these women of science
something repeating itself yes
from the stone slabs

CORINNE

A thing happened yesterday. I thought it was bath water leaking out. I was on the edge of the forest on the path I was carving out. I was in a dream on the path to my house. With every step I felt wetness between my legs. Something leaks out, sometimes, it's white, it'll come out in the wash Dame Anne used to say. It smells like the earth from the garden. I sniffed. I don't know why, but I touched the hole. I touched myself there and my fingers came out red. I went to hide between the trees. I let the trees stroke my coat, the ground swallow my boots. I don't know why, but I put a pine cone in my mouth. Unconsciously, I slipped my hand in again and I don't know. Maybe it was the pain, but I couldn't stop poking it in. The forest is a refuge. A good place to be alone with your red hand. Bleeding from this hole gave me the right to a self-examination in the solitude of the forest. Bleeding from this hole made me want to like it better. I played with myself, just for myself, and took my time.

LAURE

damedread sinks the shovel into the ground

every day yes

to see how much time is left

to feel death hee hee

DIANE

laure laure laure laure laure laure laure laure laure
laure laure laure laure laure laure laure laure laure
laure laure laure laure laure laure laure laure laure
laure laure laure laure laure laure laure laure laure
laure laure laure laure laure laure laure laure laure
laure laure laure laure laure lure laure laure laure
laure laure laure laure laure laure laure laure laure
laure laure laure laure laure laure laure laure laure
laure laure laure laure laure laure laure laure laure
laure laure laure laure laure laure laure laure laure
laure laure laure laure laure laure laure laure laure
laure laure laure laure laure laure laure laure laure
laure laure laure laure laure laure laure laure laure

JEANNE

blood in corinne's underwear
dame dominique smiles at a new woman
the washerwoman knows our uterine secrets
                             like a replacement mother
dame dominique throws out the tail
soiled by corinne

CORINNE WOULD HAVE SAID

Jeanne's hand won't heal and it's a small victory. The cut between my legs will never heal. Will return every month. Being a woman is a wound. I feel like the neighbour's dog that urinates against a tree. That tree is my tree. Jeanne and Colette are my territory.

ARIANDRE

I snapped the fly off Dame Anne's brooch. Jewellery is useless. The insect sits in the crook of my palm. I'm not good with people. I got permission to go to the library at night. Dame Gabrielle finally agreed, but I don't think she really heard me. I just took Dame Anne's key, which was hanging from a hook in her bedroom. She's young in the photos I found in her drawer. There she is, a little girl. Two adults standing next to her. A woman and a man. She looks like them. I go to the library to write. Light a small lamp in the aisle with the English novels. It's silent as the grave. I don't say a word. I look at the fly.

ANNETTE

it's when the sun slips through the branches to
light our faces hello that the worries disappear and
the sun reaches me falls on me draws me a mouth
dances in my face laure and dame dread walk from
the kitchen to the shed they take care of what's
left of dame algebra they cut her up into little balls
melon scoops the water flows away in the furious
river carries off the white pieces that chip off from
the mountains the snow melts and tells me life will
go back to how it was not long now it's not long it's
only ever a winter's length the bear tracks around
the shed it's the smell that brought it here laure
leaves her room to go to the shed and ariandre
leaves her room to go to the library watchers in
the night

LAURE

damedread has told me yes

she has taught me since i came here hee hee

my feet crossed the walls of the school

and already she looked at me like another

one of those who know

those who recognize

and who feel

i learn the knowledge of damedread

and jeanne catches the echoes

DIANE

Colette says nothing Catherine says nothing
Benoîte says nothing Frédérique says nothing
Léa says nothing Corinne says nothing Thérèse
Charlotte Sylvie Lucile Bernadette Jacinthe
Suzanne Rose-Anna Aimée and Dorothée don't
see us and soon my disappearance

JEANNE

down to the cellar
in darkness sometimes
release the prey from the predators
the eyes are everywhere yes
i am the disciple of laure and damedread
annette walks the corridors her hands brushing
                                    the wall hee hee
looking for the one with the blackened fingers

ANNETTE

if the sound is hollow it's a head and it's the head of dame gabrielle who softly beats the wooden doors a pulse that's become the norm boom if she hadn't asked laure to shovel dame anne would have fallen on a white pillow boom today the ground was thawed out we said goodbye to dame algebra placed the stone slabs on top of her memory boom i picked up an earthworm it tried to escape both ways closed up my palm for a tunnel no entry here i block its path with my finger and i block its path with my fist whistle to attract the hummingbirds gift in my hand dame gabrielle loved dame anne i saw her at the bedside of the sick leg

JEANNE

laure and damedread in the shed
plants scattered around the greenhouse
living in secret behind the rakes yes
i straighten the stone slabs that have slipped
watched by annette who keeps a lookout
ariandre at her window
laure says keep an eye on the one who writes
laure says and jeanne obeys hee hee

LAURE

the virgin eyes of damedread fixed on her hand

spit the chewed-up leaves onto corinne's path

jeanne with her endless scars

speaks of diane with her ancient pain

cut the leaves and stir the pot yes

a new friend in the shed hee hee

a friend i can read from the inside out

ANNETTE

the bear comes back to sniff the odour dame algebra's pit it dances around the pit its nose to the
ground the crazy the huge bear i watched from
my window i have this little window as everyone
has their window pane to look outside mine faces
dame algebra i see her when i wake up hello

ARIANDRE

There's one person I really want nothing to do with, and that's Annette. I already know exactly what she's thinking. Her eyes follow me. I go left, she goes left. I go to the cellar at night, she comes down the cold staircase in her stockings. I'm losing all my freedom with this shadow following me around. I can't be the spy. When someone is watching me, and I didn't choose it, all my mystery is taken away. Sometimes I attract attention, but only because I want to. Only I get to decide. Not the eyes of other people. Let me dance. I heard footsteps running in the corridor of the attic bedrooms, and a few minutes later, I saw Diane standing in her coat at the edge of the forest. Better watch out for bears. I can't stand being a character in someone else's story. Annette ought to cut out her tongue. Like the last girls.

DIANE

i'm walking in the soft damp snow a few steps
soaked through my bones are cold i am in the
wrong skin i don't understand my own face anymore something is gone the drink gave me a new
branch don't break it i've turned into a lake my
skirt is heavy and that's how it is that's the right
way lie down on the last snow that soaks through
and let myself be swallowed up in bad thoughts
frédérique was never close to me never tried to
ask questions jeanne is mystical and her words
are false ariandre looks at me and understands
she knows that something is blocked As if my
head underwater As if my body assaulted As if i
bumped against the rocks As if i drank without

121

thirst As if i drowned As if i disappeared As if i heard the wolves As if they caught my scent As if the falls As we slip between the stone slabs

ANNETTE

where are you yoohoo where did she go the
woods or the bedroom the door closed for two
days help me give me the key i want to look
through her window i am a hummingbird that
looks in through the window ariandre is invisible
in class and dame gabrielle keeps up the massacre
boom in mourning and cock-eyed doesn't notice
anymore the ones who aren't there where did
she go the bear is gone the lane has melted the
snow is hidden with the roots under the trees and
ariandre doesn't come out of her room at night
anymore not one day without her otherwise i will
crumble don't know who i boom

DIANE WOULD HAVE SAID

Melt away and be forgotten.

ARIANDRE

Through the half-open window, I threw the fly
onto the stone slabs below. Sleep well, Dame
Anne. I retreat into my closet. Lovely place. Dame
Anne is resting. Dame Gabrielle is falling apart,
and Diane has turned to liquid and gone with the
last girls. I think she needed deliverance. It's not
easy to be a prisoner of the seasons. I imagine her
drifting in the current, a smile or a look of con-
tentment on her long, oval face. We are captive
at this school. Diane closed in on herself like one
of the shells that she'll soon be among, when the
river lets out into another current. She turned in
on herself, spiralling tighter and tighter inwards
until even her face was gone. Like the last girls,

the ones we forget. It's as if they disappeared of their own accord, with no one else lifting a finger. Their once-dangling tongues were pulled out and the space has stayed empty. I've left pages in my notebooks for the new little girls and the stories they'll tell.

JEANNE

always absent yes
even when she was here
diane took the path through the woods
went with the wolves
not my fault hee hee
i only help those who are already lost
so says laure manitou

JEANNE WOULD HAVE SAID

I always help others am never a problem I throw them a line if it lashes them it's not my shadow that wants a telling-off. Jeanne becomes Laure becomes a witch as the days go by. I did not kill Diane it was my sister who slaked her thirst with the potion.

LAURE

damedread guessed hee hee

little by little

the melting snow disintegrates

we are learning algebra yes

the moment the earth rumbles

it's the forest we should have been afraid of

ANNETTE WOULD HAVE SAID

How many years will it take until I'm the right person? I am never with the others, I am always apart, perhaps the girls find me too young or too blank. That would be worse. Blankness. I am not good for making friends. I only make myself miserable. I make myself miserable by wanting to be with the others. I ought to learn to be Annette with no mirror. Keep my eyes on my hands my wings my little pin of a beak bobbing around in front of me. Stop looking for my reflection in Ariandre. Be Annette. The one without the power of events.

SUMMER

ARIANDRE

Very often, I find myself alone at the end. But that sounds as if I were among others at the start. I have always been alone. Even in the middle of a group, I'm alone. Even surrounded by children, I'm alone. Even with family, I'm alone. The people I think I love keep their distance because even with them, I'm alone. Catherine has left. Catherine left with the others. The other Catherine wouldn't have dared. Why did she disguise herself? She abandoned me behind the shed and her footprints vanished. Everyone's footprints vanish. I often used to go behind the shed, to put my feet where the other Catherine's had been. But her feet are clean now. I don't know how to make my own footprints. I don't know how to be out in the world. How to bring myself out. I don't know if the others know, either. Maybe, underneath it all, I'm just saying what everyone else is thinking, behind their closed eyes. Maybe I'm young and as I get older I'll find the answers to these mysteries. But honestly, I don't think so. I don't think that Dame Dominique knows all the answers, even if she knows how to find me behind the shed. I don't think that Dame Gabrielle knows infinity. For now, she doesn't know anything but the grain of the wood of the science classroom door. I don't think that Dame Anne knew much about the angles of the roof. I think that Dame Dread perhaps knows something that I don't know. But I also think that as soon as you know, you end up separated from everyone else, forever. That's it. I've been in my room for a week and Dame Dread has been in her cabin next to the shed for what seems like an age. No one has come knocking and I finish up wondering if everyone has disappeared. I finish up thinking that no one ever existed. I finish up thinking that it's often like that in summer. Everyone leaves and I stay. The school is my nest. I fly low. Brush against the dusty floor of the cellar. Léa has left, along with her night walks.

Every night, I open the door of my room and find a dish there. I don't know who sees me. I don't know who knows I exist. I don't understand what that dish is doing there, but I eat, and every day I put the dish back where I found it. I sharpen my pencils with a knife. Take the opportunity to pierce my skin here and there. To prove to myself that I really am here. Diane has left with her silence. The others tend to vanish. They're there, and summer comes, and they're not there anymore. The snow has melted, taking them with it. The river thunders. I hear it through the half-open window and say to myself, what a lovely grave. I let in a breath of air through the window and I walk around my room. My bed, my desk, my washbasin, my closet. It's built into the wall, gives me a little room for patience. A blank, dark space to learn how to slip away. I often go inside, closing the door behind me. I breathe in the smell of my clothes. Bury my head in them, lick the coat-hangers with their metallic taste. Often, in that space, I am empty. I like erasing myself that way. Entering the dimension of darkness. It doesn't frighten me in there, not at all. I know it well. I've touched the four corners at the top and the four corners at the bottom. I've counted the nails by the light of a candle. I know how many planks make up the floor. The texture of the walls. The knots in the wood. A few spiders. They say you swallow them in your sleep. They say, too, that spiders feed on the other small insects that live in the room. Never kill a spider. Bad luck. Rain. I feed on other people's insects. The one that lives in my head is quiet in the closet. It folds its wings, curls up its antennae, stops its buzzing. That's good. Good for me. I stay in there, sitting or standing. I think about the emptiness. Annette has left. I think that Dame Anne has perhaps been eaten by maggots. I think that the headmistress will come back. I think that Diane fell in the river and that no one will go looking for her. I think that it's better for her that she left with the snow. She can start her life again, in the river. For my part, I'm going to live in my closet for a while, then step out of my bedroom, and when I'm certain that no one else except me is living in the school, I might leave my room altogether. Take a walk in the dark hallways under the arches. Open the doors of the others' bedrooms, weigh their absence. I'll leave Annette's door closed. Frédérique has left with Benoîte and the older girls. This morning, clink of ceramic on tiles. My dish. I think there's a presence here that won't go away. I don't know that I'm surprised by that realization. I'm used to it, but at the same time, unsettled by the idea that every day, someone thinks of me. I don't believe that someone could take care of a person for so long and expect nothing in return. Jeanne has left with her face like a mime. When I open the door to pick up the dish, I don't see one in front of the others' doors. Why have they all left and not me. Why does someone still feed me. Maybe someone thinks that mine is a mouth worth feeding. It's easy to imagine when you don't go out anymore. When you stay shut in between four walls. Or inside the four top corners and the four bottom corners of the closet. It's easy to think and to imagine when you see everything through the window. I've never liked to confide. It often feels too delicate, too dangerous. I don't want others to know things about me that I don't know. When I talk, I often say too much, so I prefer to keep my mouth shut. I talked to the other Catherine but then she went and repeated things. Things I didn't say to anyone else. Things that I said for me. So it wouldn't spill over. Catherine has left with the other Catherine. I am a vase. I hold flowers. I hold water and I'm breakable. I only break when I'm struck in just the right place. I've already fallen on the ground and my edges are sharp. I've lost a few pieces. They've been thrown in the trash. Pierced everything else that was in there. Turned into a thousand tiny fragments. I find myself in all kinds of nooks and crannies. Dame Dread clears up the debris of everything. Turns it into other things. Hardly anything goes to waste at this school. I know that Dame Dread is here. She's in the walls. But she's not the one who leaves the dish at my door. I would have recognized her limping step. I would have felt her presence in the corridor. Dame Dread is not the bringer of the dish. Colette has left with her back like a doormat. This morning, the sound of ceramic on the tiles. No dish but a cup. I drink. Then I rise up my bed my desk my washbasin my closet someone has poisoned me did this person want to hurt me that's what happens with fear we believe that everyone is out to get us or that no one is out to get us that no one wants to believe us that no one can bear the sight of us we look at the world from its negative and base our whole life on the opposite on the image that is nothing without the light believe in the gloom or in the room or in the closet believe that because you go to the toilet in the washbasin no one knows what's inside your head and at the same time believe that all other voices pass through you and give you the power to know the thoughts of each one but without knowing if what you strive to dream up is real believe in the plots and then open the window to let the air in and then why not open the door and go out of the room go out in boots but no clothes because why not summer was born with the burial dame anne has left with her flies and even if the summer would normally be enough hide for a long time in the closet and finally go out and walk naked among the paintings the scene of the school in the snow was painted by benoîte she painted it and dame dominique hung it in the hallway and then i drew the school in my notebook so that i could try to make something beautiful too but i didn't show it to anyone and maybe they would have thought it was ugly or worse they would have said that i had done the same as benoîte and i don't want to do the same as the others corinne has left with her fury i go down the stairs that lead to the teachers' bedrooms a floor that looks just like ours with the room that belonged to dame anne and her last breath there is no dish in this corridor either i go down even further and it's the floor where benoîte thérèse charlotte sylvie lucile ber-nadette jacinthe suzanne rose-anna aimée and dorothée have their bedrooms they are separated from us by dame dominique dame gabrielle the late dame anne and dame françoise dame dread prefers to sleep in the shed she sleeps in a cabin next to it heated by a big stove in winter laure says the shed needs humidity i don't know why i don't want to know what they do in there once i saw laure going in and i told myself don't look inside instead i looked at the moss like i always do and at the trees standing up like posts i go into the main hall another floor down and the columns spin around me like trees and i turn a cartwheel and i do a handstand and i look at myself i look like the candles straight and beige smooth and flat i stand on my hands upside down for a long time in the main hall it's not uncommon to see a bird flying around the columns double and stretch out to infinity it reminds me of the trees they are here they have always been here there were other girls before me and one day i won't be here anymore and there will be girls after me maybe every column is a girl that never left i want to count them i run around the main hall and touch them one by one and then i run some more and touch them all but i forget to count so i start again but i forget again and i don't count i have never counted for anyone dame anne is dead maybe she would have been able to show me calculations and something other than addition i know there are other things but i wasn't listening i was thinking about the other catherine who abandoned me and about the adults who don't come to fetch me anymore when the season turns hot negligence or maybe they came and fetched the other catherine instead she's a better person than i am for many reasons dame dominique has left and soon no one will be able to stop me from staying behind the shed i feel the air coming in through my nose and the dust trembles in the corner of the wall and footsteps sound at the back of the hall i hide behind the infinite rows of columns heavy steps and no limp i can't see a thing i don't like to see when i'm afraid i prefer to hide in the folds of my dresses between the four corners at the top and the four corners at the bottom i only come out when i feel well again when my insect has calmed down right now it's calm it might even be asleep that's good for me i make a detour i go to the bathroom hold hands with the washbasin everything is cold i press down on the pedal and dip my hair under the water that turns me into a fish dame gabrielle has left with her bruised forehead boom every lump of snow that fell might have been a little girl i will fall down too if the winter comes back perhaps i will fall down if the winter comes back i will fall from the roof and break my neck or my leg i have to go out from here walk down the corridor with its narrow corners leading to the library here the books speak for themselves just fine it's a lovely place i missed it the tall windows the wooden shelves filled with books i touch the covers the dust is thick and hardened i must come back with a duster i climb up on the big table and realize that i'm naked that i have been for a while too bad it doesn't matter anyway i'm alone problems only come with other people i'm alone and that's a good thing a very good thing from the table i look at the river that twists and turns above the trees it looks tempting it looks alive i would slip right in slip my feet in slip my bare shoulders in slip right in like a fish my skin slippery join diane the classroom is empty dame dominique's classroom i push all the desks into a corner and dance to bring the wind i open the high windows the birds can come and live with me in the school robins to wake me in the morning cuckoos to feed me worms on the floor swallows to brush against my slippery skin crows to teach me mathematics huge crows and handsome black robes they would be well dressed well turned out anyway handsome blue feathers belle epoque i go into dame dominique's language classroom all i find is a rotten apple in my desk all that's hidden rots i go out again after i've thrown the apple outside apple-tree soon enough i wander down to the cellar passing by the room of the late dame anne and her fly buried under the paving stones but i'm not dead so i talk about her i make what once existed live again and sometimes i said things about others that maybe didn't exist at all made the true live alongside the false help me i'm sorry and i'm sorry i lied or i invented or i made up most of the others' words i don't know if it's bad but i have an instinct for lies and it gnaws at me it makes me ashamed have i been alone all along i imagine myself surrounded by people to survive i imagine what they're thinking to survive i imagine they talk to me and talk to each other i invent their intentions even if i don't look for the truth it's easier that way the damp hits me immediately in the cellar it's what we always feel straight away that smell in the nose that chill my nipples have gone hard i am in the walls of death next to dame anne and the last girls underground next to her she's there behind the wall that closes in around my body i go down further and still further and deeper toward the middle and past the door that felt the beating head of dame gabrielle it was there through the science classroom window i look at the place where laure stood the place where dame anne fell it's the same window laure knew the cooped-up smell is so strong that i open all the windows again the memory will disappear carry on in the darkness to the vault i steal straw-berries and raspberries swallow them delicious juice drips down to my belly-button and i'm deli-cious and i'm a strawberry i need no one to eat me i want no one to know that i'm a ripe fruit but if the strawberries are picked it means there is a woman somewhere to pick them another person that i didn't dream up a moving being with hands that pick and then i won't have made it all up and maybe i am just one of those people who has all the powers and who gives the impression of being the creator of all thoughts because she needs to maybe i'm just a person who is afraid or a person who is suffering or a person who prefers not to know a person who writes to stay away to guess in that case i'm no more than a liar and all my inventions are false and all my words a riddle and all my madness revealed and all my life i will be apart because of the fear it's out of step it's in my mind more than in my actions but maybe i am alone really alone and already i feel the monotony of the darkness in the cellar and i think about my closet again so soft about my window through which i can watch what's happening outside dame anne doesn't have to worry about anything anymore but her death and her presence under the stones did they really happen or am i having a moment of false recollection i don't know the others' names anymore but i know i hated them all it's easier always easier to hate a part of me inside them all i go back upstairs and walk across the old stones toward the dining hall perhaps the strawberry-picker is there perhaps she'll put her arms around me pick me up like a little fruit how do i know the hall is untouched no trace no eyes no girl's hair i talk about the others because i am nothing or a few sounds from the kitchen a few sounds push the door open something's bubbling in the pots something's cooking on the stove the picker was here just recently she can't be far otherwise why the food why the dish outside my door i hear her singing and she's in the garden she sings in her mountain language i don't know how to smile i don't know if it's a good thing in the end that someone is here someone feeds me a person wants my well-being a person takes care of me a person in the garden picking carrots and herbs a person with dirty hands whom frédérique saw as a substitute as a bond as something sweet and gentle but i don't have that i don't have that bond it got broken not by me not my choice they pre- ferred catherine over me or the other catherine one summer they forgot to come and fetch me my body stayed at the school dame françoise lost her daughter not her choice maybe we are alike in loss maybe i need her and she needs me but maybe she also wants to steal my body from me put her daughter inside it dame françoise looks after her daughter with my face although her daughter must have been less ugly less horrid she must have preferred her daughter even if she left never knew her adolescent i am the wrong one i am not her own i am not anybody's she feeds me but i am still the wrong one i am here and i'm not good enough it's a shame i could have been a good girl and let myself be fed but i have trouble with good manners trouble with being nice and how the world wants me to suffer i am just a bird that's afraid that flies up to the top of the tree to the highest branch to watch from far away what's happening below i escape behind the shed and stand with my boots in the moss but the moss is full of mud it wants to suck me in so i take off my boots to feed the swamp and escape barefoot into the forest the trees the pines understand me they stroke my back and make me shiver the only comforting touch and i let the roots take me and devour the black earth

LAURE

damedread hums

daughters of the cult

daughters of the occult and

yes

daughters of the forest

hee hee

QC FICTION

Current & Upcoming Books

Visit **qcfiction.com** for details and to subscribe
to a full season of QC Fiction titles.

Printed by Imprimerie Gauvin
Gatineau, Québec